A Black Butterfly's Journey Towards CLAR.R.R.ITY

Reveal Renew Reignite!

The C.E.O Woman's Inner Guide

Richale R. Reed, MA, LCMHCS, LCAS Best- Selling Author

A Black Butterfly's Journey Towards CLAR.R.R.ITY
Reveal, Renew, Reignite
The C.E.O Woman's Inner Guide
Copyright © 2020, 2025

New Large Print Edition 2025
Publisher Richale R. Reed
Imprint: Black Butterfly Way
ISBN- 978-1-7349078-2-7
Printed in the United States of America
Cover Design: Besty McElwee
Cover Photo: Christina C. Williams
Interior Art: Stacy Hummel

Unless otherwise indicated Scripture references are from the New King James Version. Copyright 1982 by Thomas Nelson, Inc. Used by permission. All rights reserved.

Scripture quotations labeled AMP
Scripture quotations labeled NIV
Scripture quotations labeled MSG

This publication is intended to provide helpful and informative material on the subjects addressed. Readers should consult their personal health care professionals before adopting any of the suggestions in this book or drawing inferences from it. The author and publisher expressly disclaim responsibility for any adverse effects arising from the use or application of the information contained in this book.

DEDICATION

This book is dedicated to every spiritual father and mother, teacher, mentor, and angel assigned to my path to offer enlightenment and truth in love; for encouraging me to live a life of authenticity and purpose through higher education, personal, professional, and spiritual development.

To those who have trusted me to support them as their therapist and coach but in actuality have been my teachers.

A special thank you to God for the mother He assigned me, who as of this 2nd edition has gone to be with the Lord. She was truly my greatest teacher in life and after life, thus our story shall be shared soon so that others might learn from her purpose in life!

Lastly, God thank you for equipping and inspiring me to write, speak, teach, and exude my thoughts in my unique voice without apology.

Foreword

The conversation started light, a brief "catching up," then a short chat about the benefits of essential oils and self- care. I hadn't planned on meeting up with my friend that day, but shortly after we began, she had opened up and was sharing her story with me. I listened intently. It was a story in which most people would have crumbled, but she shared it with brave humor and a transformational attitude. She spoke with such clarity, purpose, and resilience. It intrigued me. Both of us worked in helping professions, and as she talked, I wondered how my own story influenced my work. The more she continued, the more my mind was flooded with questions. Did I even understand my whole story? Was I resilient enough to teach those I worked with how to be resilient? Did my story connect to my God-given purpose? How would I know? My friend's transparency and conviction about how she was to use her story accomplish her life's purpose, revealed a missing connection in my own life. I left her presence that day, knowing that I was missing a vital piece to understanding and carrying out my purpose. That day, a spark was set within me to pursue the true understanding of my experiences and life's purpose.

Though this encounter deeply and personally impacted me, it was not an intimate conversation with my best friend. Instead, we were two strangers in a large auditorium. She was the presenter of the hour, and I was a simple conference attendee in an audience of hundreds of other mental health professionals. My first experience of Richale R. Reed was only an encounter for me; she didn't even know I was in the room. Although she had no knowledge of me personally, and I was just another face in the crowd, she spoke directly to a part of me that I didn't even realize was questioning. What I would come to understand is that this experience was not unique, but rather, Richale's gift to connect with individuals no matter how many people are in a room manifesting. This was just one of her many gifts that I would come to experience consistently over the years.

After that day, I began a journey to understand my God-given purpose and how my story was vital to it. That journey led me to seek out and participate in several of Richale's masterminds, group coaching experiences, conference sessions, training, online courses, and individual coaching programs. We've *now* even had several opportunities to have real one-on-one conversations. During every encounter, formal or informal, I was challenged to go within and work on myself to reach the next level of personal development.

Richale has taught me that my quest for clarity needed to be directed inward. I've since learned how to go within for answers to life's questions. I've learned that the gap between my story and my purpose could only be closed by intentionally doing my own inner work. This skill, yes, it is a skill, has resulted in clarity, resiliency, growth, and courage for me. I've learned that being clear on my life's purpose is not some haphazard occurrence or a construct predestined by fate. Nor is the answer in any outside source. I must intentionally and actively seek after it, inwardly. I am not in life's waiting room, holding my breath until my name is called from the other side of some random door to be told what would happen next. I have a choice. I am in control.

Richale's God-given essence is centered in an ability to usher people within themselves, help them tap into The Source, and create the growth they desire. Her level of transparency as a therapist, certified coach, trainer, speaker, and author will show you a glimpse of who you can be on the other side of persistent inner work. As I've grown to know Richale personally, I've been fortunate to observe her consistency and reliance on her own inner processing. I've seen the results, and they are awe-worthy. Richale is committed to her life's work and is invested in supporting others in theirs.

The undeniable truth is that we all have hopes and dreams of being significant and making an impact in this world, whether great or small. However, many times, we fall short of understanding how this is going to happen. We often find ourselves hopeless to find answers, because we've allowed doubt to take root on the inside. When we can't see why we are where we are, it's because we've allowed our insecurities to obscure our vision. When we don't bounce back from life's blows, it's because we cannot see how life's experiences are on our path to significance and purpose. The problem is that we look for others to come and rescue us and for unfavorable circumstances to change for the better. My prayer is that you allow Richale, through the pages of this book, to reveal the truth and connect to that part of you that is longing for answers. I pray that as you read this 2nd Edition Large Print with QR codes to some powerful tools, you are convinced that all you need and want is

INside of you, and you just have to work it OUT. So, get your cup of tea, a notebook (trust me, you'll need it), and prepare for a life-changing conversation with my, and your soon-to-be favorite therapist, coach, and sister-friend, Richale.

Alexis Wester, M.Ed., LCMHC, NCC

CONTENTS

DEDICATION..3

Foreword..4

CONTENTS 9

PREFACE...10

GROUND ZERO 15

CHOOSE 24

LOVE..50

ACT 60

THE TRIPLE R EFFECT 74

IAMNESS...83

TOOLS 94

YIELD 103

FINAL WORDS 111

ABOUT THE AUTHOR…........................114

MORE FROM THE AUTHOR………...……116

PREFACE

Many years ago, this book was inspired out of my growing understanding of how integral it is to guard one's heart and mind (Proverbs 4:23-27). This understanding came from my studies of my favorite book, *The Bible*, coupled with challenging life experiences I overcame, followed by my aspiration to higher education and becoming a licensed clinical mental health therapist and addictions specialist. As a result, I now see life through a different lens, colored by countless clients who have allowed me to journey alongside them as the voice of clarity—hereafter referred to using the mnemonic CLAR.R.R.ITY, a process that guides them to their places of CLAR.R.R.ITY and transformation.

Today, this book was birthed, as the climate of our nation is increasingly "panicked" about its future. Panic is the sudden presence of uncontrollable fear and anxiety, which often causes "wildly unthinking behavior," according to the Oxford dictionary. What is important to understand about panic is that *panic, generally, does not begin outwardly but inwardly as it is a mental and emotional disturbance of the mind attached to one's future.* This is primarily, why in my professional opinion, anxiety-induced situations occur far more than depressive ones due to the attack on future thinking versus the past where depression is rooted. Anxiety, on a clinically impaired level, is merely an irrational projection of the uncertainty of one's future. Panic, as such, is rooted in anxiety, and it gains power as a result of what we feed our minds through our ear gates and eye gates. These are the windows of our souls, which eventually enslave us mentally if not protected. It then projects itself; thus, coloring our world grey with the falsehood that our futures are in jeopardy of reaching infinite potential; the believer's birthright. As a result, CLAR.R.R.ITY is lost and panic continues to wreak havoc until it takes over our bodies, thereby holding us captive physiologically, psychologically, and spiritually. *If not careful, we could hold the key to the freedom of our future in our hands, yet allow panic to hold us captive.* For those who have ever felt unsure about their future, the answer to this imprisonment is found in our responsibility to nurture the fertile fields of the beautiful minds we have been gifted with. Moreover, it is our responsibility to go within because "where the spirit of the Lord is there is liberty" (2 Corinthians 3:17).

It is my goal to share my experiences, wisdom, and clinical expertise with *C.E.O* **women**, that is, women *Conquering Everyday Obstacles* like yourself. I will do so in a way that you cannot only digest but absorb, allowing it to nurture your subconscious mind where true transformation takes root. Doing so will call for re-examining our perspectives as it relates to what we have been taught to believe through mainstream sources of education and religion. It is also my goal to equip you with the knowledge to develop your true nature and potential so that you can lead in the marketplace you were called to.

With that said, I suggest that the best way to absorb the material in this new edition-large print is one chapter at a time. I would suggest no more than a week go by before the next chapter is begun. Before you get too far in your reading, I recommend you STOP right now and access/download the **Black Butterfly's Tool Box right here!** You are going to love this and all the artwork inside. It will be referenced as **BBTB** from here on out.

It is meant to stretch and grow you. You will find the **mind-shift exercises** that correspond with each given chapter, which are practical and inspiring tools that will coach you to your next level. I am not only a certified coach but a therapist, and I want to be clear that the mind-shift exercises are not intended for deep-seated clinical issues without the support of a licensed professional; to include the **Triple R Effect.** You are advised, if you have deep psychological concerns, to seek a loving professional faith-based counselor or therapist to help you transform.

Furthermore, read the book for yourself and for someone you love; that means even if you don't feel like it applies to you, consider it a takeaway that you can share for discussion with a sister C.E.O. However, if your sister wants your copy, be quick to bless her with one or tell her to get her own! Lastly, you will find each chapter has its own flow; no cookie-cutter pattern here. However, you will consistently find a mix of CLAR.R.R.ITY questions, scripture references, and quotes meant to inspire new thinking in each chapter and your toolbox holds all those questions and more.

My hope is that you use this book as a tool to come out of the fog of not knowing who you are and what you are capable of, if only you would dare to take a deep dive inside to unlock the hidden treasure that is uniquely you. Moreover, I hope that collectively, we as women, take our place as nature's nurturers. That we intentionally engage in the process of restoring an environment of calm by taking back our minds with the tools found within us. Tools which were given us to till the fertile grounds of our minds, essentially bringing back into existence the certainty of a luminous future for the generations that will come through us. We will transform our lives and the world when we lead from one glorious example to another, which only comes as a result of the journey traveled from within.

0
GROUND ZERO
The Gift of Ground Zero

"Ground Zero," two words that remind us of one of the greatest tragedies in American history, and as I write this book, we have entered yet another such time. Having never experienced the level of devastation as we did on 9/11, as a nation with the world looking on, it was hard to imagine how we would survive it individually and collectively. It was simply unimaginable, surreal, and traumatizing. In fact, it was life-changing.

As I write this book, we are once again witnessing an event never seen before; that is, the genesis of a new virus known as the coronavirus or COVID-19, which has reached "pandemic" proportions according to most media sources. **However, if you are reading this post-pandemic, keep reading!** It's said to have affected 184 countries as of Easter Sunday morning. *The New York Times* live updates newsfeed on Easter Sunday suggests that as of Saturday, 16 million Americans were out of work. This same report claims that as of Easter Sunday, 20,500 people have succumbed to the deadly virus. In attempts to stop the spread of disease and continued loss of life, Easter services are being live-streamed as churches, schools, and businesses across the country and globe are shut down. Most states are under stay-at-home orders with curfews in place. No one but essential workers can work, and six-foot social distancing regulations isolate family members, neighbors, and worshippers alike. Many working from home simply feel imprisoned as it's often referred to as "lockdown." Unfortunately, a natural effect of this "pandemic" is a crashing stock market, the loss of wages, reduction of hours, layoffs, furloughs mostly unpaid, small and large businesses in sudden economic hardship, and massive assistance requests.

Our president at the time of this original writing, Donald Trump and his cabinet, along with bi-partisan federal and state support, have responded resoundingly to address the needs of Americans through stimulus checks, economic hardship loans, and grants to help employers keep their employees for a short time as the nation waits for a decline in the spread of this plague that is responsible for over 100,000 deaths in the U.S., and counting.

In order to stay relevant, small, medium, and large enterprises are turning to video conferencing software to remain present in the marketplace. While other industries failed overnight, we witnessed industries from school systems to healthcare systems to media outlets rely totally on telecommunication operations such as Skype, Zoom, and Google Meet to render services. Thus, we now have a surge in the tech industry but not without its share of problems due to being unprepared for the large demands. Amongst the strangest change of events were celebrity musicians and DJs hosting free concerts from their living rooms. At the same time, comedians told jokes from their respective studios with no live audience. Spiritual leaders were neither exempted as they streamed their preaching from the pulpits of empty churches or their homes, including holy events such as Passover and Resurrection services. More concerning is families and friends having no choice but to connect using these same methods. I, even, celebrated my sister's birthday through an Alexa video call and organized a sort of family reunion with my extended family through Zoom.

Due to the pandemonium of fear, toilet papers, Lysol, and other cleaning supplies are now scarce, and there is little to no food on the shelves. Filters to protect our healthcare workers and everyday citizens are being sold at unreasonable prices despite threats to prosecute price gougers at the onset of the pandemic. Most unsettling is that despite age, race, culture, gender, class, and socioeconomic status, there are rising incidences of domestic violence and overall trauma to American citizens due to the increased anxiety, anger, lack of control, and effects of being caged. Unfortunately, this is a trend that mental health professionals are tracking in real-time from other countries that were affected by the coronavirus before the United States. Americans are in a panic mode because there are no experts when it comes to this disease. Many feel helpless and hopeless, which I see as a great opportunity to discover the gift in a ground-zero experience.

As you read this book, it is important that you take inventory of the condition of your heart and mind. Take cognizance of your station in life before you proceed, and be honest with yourself. My reasoning is simply that in order to execute the ideas and spiritual-mind exercises presented in this book, there has to be a basic understanding and agreement about your source as compared to the Source. **I have mastered many roles, acquired many valuable things and accomplished much, but my mastery, acquisition, and accomplishment speak to what but not necessarily who I am. Who I am, more important than anything, is a woman of God. God is the source of my supply, and that is my "Ground Zero."** The ideas that I will present to you are based on the Word of God. It is relevant to my clinical education and knowledge, as well as my physical and spiritual experience of being, in the areas of mindset and the overcomer's life!

In essence, the basic understanding is that the CLAR.R.R.ITY you seek is found through a perpetual process of gaining the mind of Christ and living a life inside of Christ. *1 Peter 1:13; KJV says, "Wherefore gird up the loins of your mind, be sober, and hope to the end for the grace that is to be brought unto you at the revelation of Jesus*

Christ." Romans 8:10; NLT says, "And Christ lives within you, so even though your body will die because of sin, the Spirit gives you life because you have been made right with God.

My career has been spent investing in women like you—successful in your own right, high powered, high achieving, highly driven, passionate, yet unfulfilled, dissatisfied, dis-eased, tired, and stuck in a cycle of inner conflict. On the outside: "It's all good," you tell everyone, yet deep within, there's a disturbance. Do you desire more but you get overwhelmed with that thought? Are you tired of fronting that it's all good? Do you struggle with your real identity? Do you need CLAR.R.R.ITY of purpose? Are you stuck due to the expectations of being a one-woman show? Are you tired of doing it alone and on your own? Is it hard to see and admit that you need help? Do you sometimes think you don't deserve help? Or do you wonder if anyone is willing to help you? These doubts and unanswered questions can become hindrances to the CLAR.R.R.ITY you seek. These hindrances show up as choices to operate as unbelievers without faith, believers whose faith is small (doubters), and believers stuck in sin consciousness (unforgiveness). Regardless of where you find yourself right now, there is help and there is hope! Although God wants the best for you and me, God will never force a choice on you. You get to **CHOOSE** if you are going to allow me to support you now. Know that everything you have right now is what you chose. Are you ready to make some new choices?

If you have not yet done so, take a minute to take inventory of your heart and mind. Where are you right now? Be honest. Now, write a statement that displays the desires of your heart, where you want to be, and make a choice.

The gift of a ground-zero experience is another chance to choose to be awakened of humanity's need for the Savior, not only in crisis but in every area and every day of our lives. If you are going to excel in life while simultaneously experiencing the peace of God, it will be because you embraced the newest opportunity to intentionally connect to THE SOURCE of power—that is, Jesus Christ.

Regardless of where you found yourself, in order for us to successfully take this journey together, with me as your coach, I offer you the knowledge of the gift of forgiveness. **Isaiah 43:25 says, "I AM He who blots out your transgressions for my own sake, and I will not remember your sins."** If you need to, ask for it now, then believe you've received forgiveness!

You just made a life-changing choice! Now, you are ready to journey through the pages of this book being introduced to a mnemonic that refers to the topic of clarity; to be referenced as **C.L.A.R.R.R.I.T.Y.** Moreover, the overarching intent is to introduce you to my process of transforming pain into purpose as well as the lives of those who have entrusted me as their therapist and coach. The entire process is a process within a process; that is seven life applications for a lifestyle of CLAR.R.R.ITY. You will find that within those seven life applications are three life applications I call **The Triple R EFFECT**. These three life applications can stand alone to aid you in the process of using the mind of Christ to manage negative thinking, increase CLAR.R.R.ITY in the moment, and improve overall mind management.

Now that we have that taken care of, and you've accepted God's forgiveness, will you now forgive yourself? You see, it is the continued condemnation of yourself (sin consciousness) that is counter-productive to this process you've decided to begin. Romans 8:1 reminds us, ***"There is therefore now no condemnation to them which are in Christ Jesus, who walk not after the flesh, but after the Spirit."*** My desire for you is to experience the power that comes from exercising the mind of Christ and enjoying life in Him. You may have to forgive yourself ten times over and that is fine. Do it, rinse, and repeat. If you believe you need more support, contact a loving faith-based counselor licensed in your state of residence or a coach with that background as there are no boundaries imposed by licensure. Know today, you are forgiven and you don't have to continue to C.E.O alone.

1
CHOOSE
CHOOSE LIFE INSIDE OF CHRIST

"Richale, if you fail to go within, you will go without!"

Always looking to serve others with impact, I chose to add certification as a John Maxwell-certified speaker, trainer, and coach. I was so excited to attend my first International Maxwell Certification conference when I met my mentor, Christian Simpson, who spoke those powerful words to me: "Richale, if you fail to go within, you will go without!" It was as if he had peeked into my soul and knew what I needed to do to shake and awaken my spirit. As a Licensed Clinical Mental Health Counselor Supervisor and Addictions Specialist with a proven track record of bringing others to a place of CLAR.R.R.ITY, these words would stir something on the inside of me, bringing a need for increased CLAR.R.R.ITY in my life. These words illuminated my path. I chose to explore "within" for the answers, hence compelling me to share this body of work with the world in a way that lights a path for you. I intend to increase your level of awareness regardless of where you are presently in life as to your understanding of "life inside of Christ."

Would you agree that to fully understand choosing a life in Christ, you need to acknowledge what life is outside of Christ? Let me be frank by telling you that I could care less to imagine what my life would be like if it were not rooted and grounded in Christ today. However, I didn't always live life inside of Christ; thus, I can remember what that was like all too well. Quite frankly, it's that memory that helps me remain grounded. Life outside of Christ for me was outside of love for myself and others, outside of joy, outside of peace, outside of CLAR.R.R.ITY, and outside of hope. Outside of Christ, I was a victim of child sexual abuse and now I am a victor. Outside of Christ, I stayed angry and now I have peace. Outside of Christ, I was hopeless, but inside of Christ, I have hope! Outside of Christ, I thought to end my life, yet inside of Christ, I know I have a purpose to fulfill! I am telling you, my life was a train wreck without Christ! However, I learned

Romans 8:28 early in my walk with Christ, that is, **"And we know that God causes all this to work together for the good of those who love God and are called according to his purpose."** This scripture became my comfort as well as a technique I personally use, which I will teach you.

Today, I am the C.E.O of a successful private practice, a licensed counselor and addictions specialist, a coach, an advisor to women and men on many paths, a wife, daughter, sister, and friend who has peace of mind, joy, and hope. I possess all these because of Christ in me, the hope of Glory (Colossians 1:27)!

I feel it necessary to make this one CLARRRIFICTION, a life inside of Christ is not an exemption from hardship and uncertainty. It means that you have inner power, authority, and strength to overcome hardship and uncertainty because of *Christ in YOU and YOU in HIM* (1 Colossians 1:13; Matthew 28:18-19). That's why I need you to stop again and consider your position. I get it; you have been successful in life. You've been able to accomplish climbing the corporate ladder and likewise become the first in your family to go and earn a degree. You've even strived to become the C.E.O of your own company and more. I say, "*Congratulations!*"

However, all the accomplishments and accolades mean nothing, in my opinion, without Christ. The way you know it matters is when you still feel void of purpose and meaning in life. If you take a quick self-inventory and find that you are dissatisfied despite your accomplishments, and you yearn for more, maybe I can help. But before you and I go any further, I am going to ask you a crucial question that will determine if you will finish this book, how you will finish this book, and why you will finish this book.

Let me explain the importance of that question. I believe that coaching should be a conscious decision and agreement between the coach and the one being coached. The coach must ask this question as the agreement comes with the responsibility to "do no harm," which is a great mandate. Although coaching is not a therapeutic relationship, it is similar in that it does require boundaries and limits that honor the relationship. I want you to know that I count it an honor, if permitted, to coach you to increased CLAR.R.R.ITY.

As your coach, I need permission to push you into thinking about topics, concepts, and ideas about yourself and your possibilities, not your current circumstances. Coaching moves you into thinking about your possibilities and what is available to you. Coaching is a function of intentional thinking mixed with faith and culminating with action. I coach using thought-provoking questions that might be uncomfortable for you at times, but with support, it can have many benefits. My responsibility as your coach is not to make you feel comfortable; it's to support you through the discomfort. I tell my clients all the time; God is not concerned about your comfort. I don't mean to sound harsh but it's true. He didn't promise us that we would not experience pain. He promised that He is faithful and has a way to support us through it (1 Corinthians 10:13).

As your coach, there will be other times I will need your permission to challenge you to avoid saying, "I don't know." I have been known to charge a quarter for every "I don't know" to challenge the client to move outside of the conscious mind into the subconscious mind. I have had the pleasure of coaching all levels of C.E.O women who were visibly frustrated by one question they just could not seem to answer in session. In response, I simply shared with them my expectation that they would **"Ask, Seek, and Knock"** until they "knew" what they "did not know" before. **"Ask, Seek, and**

Knock" is the process of exploring the kingdom of resources within you by directly connecting to Christ in you, seeking the wisdom to know thyself (Matthew 7:7-8; 1 Peter 1:3; Psalm 139:23). If you find yourself here, simply sit with yourself, starting with what you already know. Be patient with yourself, and consider taking a break. When you choose, resume marinating on the CLAR.R.R.ITY question,

"What do I already know?"

Avoid beating yourself up and enter the process of asking, seeking, and knocking and expect that the insight you need will come. It will come. Just don't give up!

You see, this Black Butterfly has been through the coaching process many times over as the coach and as the one being coached. Yes, a good coach worth their salt has also been coached. Although I came to understand the power of coaching later in life; today, I see it as an investment in myself and in those I serve. I have been blessed to have access to the voice, direction, and wisdom of highly skilled and powerful coaches whose lives were evident of a life inside of Christ. From my experience, coaching is an incubator for my accelerated personal, professional, and spiritual growth. Moreover, coaching has increased my impact on both my coaching and therapeutic practices. I know, from experience, the power of the coaching process when you go all in and hold nothing back.

In order to answer the question of your coachability, I suggest you take a look at yourself through the guise of the acronym **CHICA-TV** which outlines six qualities I believe are required to enter the coaching relationship with purpose.

CHICA-TV is the reality that takes place when you take action by saying "YES!" to the process. It is similar to reality TV shows when the stars forgot that the cameras were rolling, thereby allowing their authentic selves to show up. That is when the work can really begin.

CLAR.R.R.ITY question:
"Are you coachable?"

Choice – *Am I ready to make a choice?*

An act of your free will to emphatically choose to enter into a coaching relationship.

Humility – *Am I ready to humbly enter IN a new way?*

An act of sitting at the feet of another "flawed and jacked up" human being, surrendering to their potential to help you reach yours. Laying down your titles, degrees, talents for opportunities to go deeper, higher, and wider together.

Intention & Investment – *Am I willing to invest with intention?*

An act of deliberate engagement requiring one's time, money, and energy for the purpose of personal, professional, and spiritual development.

Commitment – *Am I willing to commit?*

An act of engaging in the process, purposing to take every opportunity to think deeper, higher, and wider.

Acceptance of Feedback – *Am I willing to accept feedback?*

An act of being open to constructive feedback.

Trust – *Do I trust my coach?*

An act of faith in that what you have not seen in the coach is congruent with what you have seen and based your "YES" on.

Vulnerability – *Am I willing to be vulnerable?*

An act of rendering your mind, will, thoughts, and emotions naked before your coach.

So, "Will you allow me to coach you?"

Again, I am honored and excited for you. You will find that powerful CLAR.R.R.ITY questions are mainly open-ended, which activates both the conscious and subconscious, allowing for deeper exploration and promotion of new thinking required for growth. Intentionally ponder on each question, and take your time to write your answers out, so as to allow for increased mastery, follow up, and accountability.

CLAR.R.R.ITY questions:
> *Have you experienced significance?*
> *Imagine it…what would significance look like for you? What's in the way of you reaching significance?*
> *Now what? What's next?*

How was that experience for you? There are many possible scenarios, and I will cover a few. Whether you were pleasantly surprised by your answers or uninspired, avoid minimizing the fact that you took the first step. If you were unable to articulate the "it" of wanting more, consider being "OK" with that for now because if you have never experienced significance, it makes sense that it would be difficult to articulate, right? Conversely, maybe you have experienced significance, yet there are new directions and experiences ahead that you don't quite have CLAR.R.R.ITY on. Consider being "OK" with that for now as well; it will come. Perhaps you find yourself unmotivated, consider if you have been so comfortable with settling for success that you feeling unfulfilled is but a mere symptom of your complacency. Lastly, is it possible that you are in a state of twisted self-delusion and now are in the throes of keeping up appearances in a most inauthentic and self-sabotaging way?

I have seen that scenario play out through countless clients that I have worked with. I am sure you know the woman that's always put together, not a hair out of place, makeup on fleek, and looking flawless! She seems happy, doesn't complain, is very accommodating, quite articulate, and seems never to make a mistake. Yet, the truth is, she is at my door because she is running on empty, exhausted, conflicted, and dazed. She is tired of numbing the pain of simply existing, tired of "faking it till she makes it," and "tired of being sick and tired." At the root, she actually is in this state of a twisted self-delusion due to feelings of inadequacy that causes her to overcompensate. What's irrational is that she has the receipts to prove that she is intelligent; yet, she has convinced herself that she is not. In fact, she is confident that the only way to be smart is to _act as if_ she is. That's a twisted self-delusion if I have ever seen one. Sadly, the moment she is found alone to sit with herself, she berates all of her accomplishments, reducing them to nothingness. This has become her reality. Due to her two-faced mastery, she vacillates from pumping herself up with man-made constructs such as rehearsing affirmations of self and positive thinking to accepting defeat as a self-proclaimed "imposter" and a "fraud," all of which have little to no effectiveness. Could this be you in totality or part? Are you failing miserably, striving to attempt this irrational state of being and beating yourself up?

You are looking into the life of a woman who has been broken, bruised, and traumatized by her experiences, with her thought-life continuing to keep record. She may have been through legitimate hell and back. Still, she can learn to discontinue self-inflicting pain from a distorted worldview that perpetuates an identity crisis through a mind that is under corrupt management. Would you agree that she is in a quandary? It's clear that she needs CLAR.R.R.ITY, right?

The problem is that she's been tending to symptoms by putting a Band-Aid on her elbow when the root problems are found in her heart and mind. This is clearly an external symptom of an internal problem. In helping my clients, of all faiths, with solving problems of internal nature, I look to the Word of God for the solution. I believe the solution is found in Matthew 5:8 (MSG) which says, *"You're blessed when you get your inside world—your mind and heart—put right. Then you can see God in the outside world."* In other words, *"When your outside world is not right, check your inside world!"*

> *You're blessed when you get your inside world—your mind and heart—put right. Then you can see God in the outside world." In other words, "When your outside world is not right, check your inside world!*

She is suffering from an inability to see God as The Source to every need she has, especially her identity crisis. She does not know her authority in Christ because she is not living inside of Christ. So, she has to gain CLAR.R.R.ITY but not without making a choice first! And she must choose because if she doesn't, she continues the dual thinking that was the genesis of a fractured mind (Luke 9:23). I must add briefly, the *mind* referenced here and throughout cannot be contained, and it must not be confused with the brain which is the matter or construct that holds the mind. If she does not choose, she will face the dire consequences of neglecting this fragile state of being, including the hindrance of personal, professional, and spiritual growth. If growth is hindered, then the production of fruit ceases to exist. She will further perpetuate a reactive state of crisis management instead of a proactive state of mind management through the mind of Christ. Existing inside of a constant state of reactivity explains her presentation of exhaustion. Our mind, body, and spirit are not designed to maintain that level of "high alert" day after day.

Hear me; it matters less how you arrived here and more about your decision to stay here. I always tell my clients: "You Can't Stay Here! God requires you to grow!" If your situation is going to change, you must shift into the mind of Christ, honing your energy, increasing CLAR.R.R.ITY, and beginning the process of producing the desired fruit of change. When that mind-shift happens in my clients, I can hear change before I can see change, and it sounds like a woman no longer stuck in the story of "what happened to me," to a woman committed to "what can I do as a result of what happened to me to help others?" This is the process of transforming the pain into purpose, transforming that pain to the highest good for yourself and those you serve. Now, that's producing fruit! You and I were created to produce fruit; that is, we were created for impact in this world (John 15:8).

In short, if you desire to begin healing, **Acknowledge, Choose, Guard, & Speak.** First, acknowledge your life inside of Christ (John 15:1-27). You then choose to heal through the power of your divinity (2 Chronicles 7:14-15). Next, actively guard your heart and mind because you will never outlive what you think about yourself; for as a woman thinketh, so is she (Proverbs 23:7). Lastly, speak the Word only over your life (Proverbs 12:14), owing to the fact that you reap what you sow in word and deed (Galatians 6:7-9). This process is integral because new thinking comes after prolonged marinating and promoting the transfer from the mind of God to your mind and heart, which eventually comes out of your mouth (Luke 6:45).

CLAR.R.R.ITY question:
> ***"What have you been thinking,***
> ***believing, and confessing about***
> ***yourself, your life, and your current***

situation, and how has that impacted your journey to significance?"

Absolutely the most influential coach I've been blessed to have in my life is my spiritual father, Pastor J.C Hash Sr. He is the first to challenge me with the idea that living life inside of Christ meant a shift from my carnal mind to my spirit mind—from the conscious mind of limitation to the subconscious mind of no limits! Pastor Hash. Sr. always said this in his prayer without fail, **"In Christ I live, in Christ I move, and in Christ I have my being!"** Interestingly, it is now part of my prayer life! This powerful confession clearly boasts of life in Christ, meaning without Him, there is no life. This bold confession confirms a knowing of where your strength comes from to be who you are and do what you were purposed to do.

See, if you don't know where your SOURCE is, you will exhaust yourself trying to make things happen instead of making your desires welcome. If you get a hold of this confession, it will negate the exhaustion, inner conflict, and even resentment that comes from you overcompensating by trying to be someone you are not or overextending yourself trying to be everything to everyone. Subsequently, it will negate the conflict that comes with the dual roles you operate from. You know the mask of being one person at home and another person at work. Exhausting, right? Does this explain why you constantly find yourself searching for reserve to fulfill the commitments you have made as you try to conquer everyday obstacles (C.E.O)? This powerful confession of faith means that you can choose to surrender to living, doing, and being all in your own strength! So, let's unpack the confession, "In Christ I live, move, and have my being!"

GET READY TO LIVE- MOVE- BE IN CHRIST!

LIVE

This is your conviction: that your life is SO inside of Christ that all that matters to you is only what matters because of who Christ is in you! So, when you reach a moment where you doubt, or you're uncertain, and you feel void of hope, you can tap into where hope comes from; that is, "Christ in you the hope of Glory" (Colossians 1:27)! Your hope should not be within yourself; your hope, my hope, and our hope should be in Christ. If my hope was in my best personality on my best day, my talents, skills, and all of my abilities, I would have a great reason to be scared because I am "flawed and jacked up!" You heard me right, and so are you! I'm not confessing I am "a fraud," but that "I am flawed!" There is a difference!

Think of your last encounter with a woman who perpetrated the fraud by **intentionally** misrepresenting her talents, skills, and abilities with the purpose of deceiving you and others for her personal gain. You'll agree that it takes a lot of energy for her to attempt to be someone she is not? However, what is evident here is that her life is rooted in a lie about who and whose she is, so her behavior and choices are congruent with the lie! What you see here is a woman whose fear is rooted in not being good enough, so she pretends to be someone who she believes is. Her focus is on what she believes she does not have; her deficits or faults.

Now, think of the C.E.O woman conquering everyday obstacles that you admire the most, who you have spent time with personally, and you know her well. You know her background story that it's not always been easy for her, but she is not stuck in that story. You know her to be faithful, passionate, virtuous, encouraging, admirable, confident in who she is, desiring to make an impact, and she does not take herself too seriously. She's learned that if she makes a mistake, she must own it, get it right, and keep it moving. What you are witnessing here is a woman that is not a "fraud" but "flawed," and she knows that she is still in the process of being perfected. Her focus is on her faith, not her faults! That's it. **Focus on your faith, not your faults.**

What I am proposing is that the first woman chose to live outside of Christ due to a belief rooted in "I AM NOT GOOD ENOUGH!" This compelled her to spend her life pretending to be someone who she imagined *was* good enough, thereby deliberately deceiving herself and others. Sin consciousness is at the root of the life outside of Christ, which can lead to irreparable damage and grave consequences or repercussions. The C.E.O woman, on the other hand, chooses to live inside of Christ, activate Christ-consciousness, and allow acknowledgment of her flaws without debasing herself. When you decide to live inside of Christ, you choose a life that brings glory to God through you! Living inside of Christ is a lifestyle that you exude because you are convinced that without Christ, life is void of meaning and purpose. Christ gives you a reason for living despite life's obvious challenges, and you will have purpose, meaning, and ultimate significance in life.

MOVE

This is the daily navigating of life in this world through the mind of Christ (1 Corinthians 2:16; Philippians 2:5). Your ability to conquer everyday obstacles will be directly influenced by your ability to overcome the dual struggle of living life as a human being versus a spiritual being. It's the argument of science versus faith that has long existed, where science proposes that we are mere neurons. However, faithful scientists and researchers have now proposed that we are created in His image and thus, a part of the whole of God that cannot be reduced as such (Genesis 1:27). In fact, those were Christians' final words to me, "Richale, you are a part of the whole!" At that moment, it seemed as if I had no idea what he meant, but I wanted to know. I needed to know, so I began searching the Scriptures. I began to ask, seek, & knock for the door of knowledge to be opened (Matthew 7:7-8). What I rediscovered is that you and I, though earthly residents, are living in a temporary state not to be prioritized above our spiritual heritage (2 Corinthians 4:7)! EVER!

With that said, there are still many cunning ways that this struggle with duality shows up for the faithful C.E.O women; for example, as mentioned earlier, the struggle known as work/life balance. Every C.E.O woman has encountered this at one time or another, mostly without understanding what is actually taking place. Do you wear two faces, one for home and the other for work because you are afraid to represent God in your decision making at work? Does anyone even know you are a woman of faith at work? Or is that not your place? Finally, are you making conscious intentional decisions or conscious intentional excuses for not serving God? This is what I know—your words, deeds, and decision-making ability should remain congruent with the mind of Christ regardless of where you are or who you are with. It is when you decide not to acknowledge God in your decisions due to your title, position, or the opinion of others who do not believe, that you choose a dual mindset that causes double-mindedness, instability, and death. James 1:5-8 (NLT) clearly explains,

"If you need wisdom, ask our generous God, and He will give it to you. He will not rebuke you for asking. But when you ask Him, be sure that your faith is in God alone. Do not waver, for a person with divided loyalty is as unsettled as a wave of the sea that is blown and tossed by the wind. Such people should not expect to receive anything from the Lord. Their loyalty is divided between God and the world, and they are unstable in everything they do."

It is best that when you move, you do so by following "the Spirit's leading in every part of" your life (Galatians 5:25; NLT). This requires a relationship with the Holy Spirit who is here to comfort, teach, guide, and lead you (John 14:26; 16:13). To develop a relationship with the Holy Spirit, you must pray (1 Thessalonians 5:17); that is, you must have an intentional dialogue with your trusted friend, comforter, and advisor. Also, allow me to add that it does not always mean you're the one doing the talking. I have learned that there is a listening side of prayer. If you are not exercising your faith, authority, and building a relationship through prayer, you will struggle to boldly confess, "In Christ I live, move, and have my being!"

As a faithful C.E.O woman, you can further avoid duality by embracing your triune nature and ability to be led by the Spirit. You must realize now that you are a spiritual being with access to the mind of Christ through the faculties of intuition and imagination, which is a function of the subconscious mind. This access to the mind of Christ is also known as (SQ) or Spiritual Intelligence. This is where your treasure is, and not in the lies of your intellect, known as your (IQ), where you can have limited access to the faculty of reasoning; a function of the conscious mind. Though the intellect is needed, the caveat again is that it should not be prioritized over the power of your spirit-mind which must be developed with intention. Remember this, where you have a natural disadvantage; for example (IQ); you have a spiritual advantage (SQ) which gives you overcoming power (1 John 4:4; 1 John 5:4; Romans 8:37). Moreover, it is through accessing the mind of Christ in all your decision making that allows you to enter what I call an "ebb and flow," where things appear to come easily to you. You will begin to experience "effortless effort" in the areas that God has purposed for you because you have been equipped with all you need to bring God's glory from heaven to earth (2 Peter 1:3).

BE

Now, this is a powerful place to "BE." This is where you will reside once you have learned how to rest in Christ, where you are free to "be" who you are authentically and without apology. This is you manifesting your triune existence, where the totality of mind, body, and spirit align with the image of God we were created in. Here, your awareness is constantly increasing (Genesis 1:27). This is where you make an agreement with your spiritual heritage, living it, moving and vibrating in it, and now expressing it through your life. There is something beautiful here that I must acknowledge: you and I share the same spiritual DNA, yet we're created intentionally to be different and that is to be celebrated. You see, even though we both were created in His image and likeness, you must own your uniqueness outright (Psalm 139:13-14). Don't waste your time or energy competing with the idea of being superior or inferior to anyone. Instead, choose to embrace that you are uniquely you (1 Peter 4:10-11)! You will find that your vibe is steady here and speaks of a woman who is "becoming," and that vibe peaks at "IAMNESS!"—a construct so crucial that it has its own chapter! For now, marinate on this prose found in Psalms 139:14-16 (MSG):

Oh yes, you shaped me first inside, then out;
you formed me in my mother's womb.
I thank you, High God—you're breathtaking!
Body and soul, I am marvelously   made! I
worship in adoration—what a creation!
You know me inside and out,
you know every bone in my body;
You know exactly how I was made, bit by bit,
how I was sculpted from nothing into
something.
Like an open book, you watched me grow from
conception to birth; all the stages
of my life were spread out before you,

The days of my life all prepared
before I'd even lived one day.

Sister C.E.O, you are fearfully and
wonderfully made! God shaped you from the
inside out, and from the inside out, you will
have life and have it in abundance!

2
LOVE
CHOOSE TO LOVE YOURSELF THROUGH THE PROCESS

"Love is a choice to recognize the author of Love within you and express that love in the world!"

Where would we be without love? Simply put, love is the reason we exist. If you were raised in the faith from an early age, you likely learned John 3:16, which says, **"For God so loved the world that he gave his one and only Son, that whoever believes in him shall not perish but have eternal life."** This is the foundation of our faith; it is the greatest example of love that there is. Think about it, you have a starring role in the greatest love story of all times and with that role comes the responsibility to, in turn, express God's love for you in the earth. That is why I believe that love is a choice to recognize the Author of Love within you and express that love in the world. Yet, why is it that we struggle with who to love, what to love, when to love, and how to love? Dare we ask, "Why love?"

When we "live a life filled with love, following the example of Christ," we bring a "pleasing aroma to God" (Ephesians 5:2; NLT). Now, because the very topic of love is as expansive as the essence of God, who is the love-giver Himself, I want to simply focus on answering this question, **"How is it that we can fulfill our responsibility to express God's love in the earth?"**

Countless C.E.O women have admitted to me of doubting whether God truly loves them for several reasons. I will share with you a few of these instances as well as my own experience with these **faulty belief systems,** also referred to as **"BS."** You understand why. As always, as you read, be honest with yourself about your thought life. Take care to identify whether any of these faulty belief systems are a part of your past or current conditioning. Remember, you cannot change what you will not acknowledge, and you will never outperform what you believe about yourself. So, I've laid a foundation for God's immense love for you; now, let's unpack the BS!

BS #1 "I guess I am still paying for what I did as a teenager" or "God couldn't love me with all the mistakes that I have made."

Does this sound like you, doubting God's love for you due to the "bad choices" you believe you have made in your life?

Love, you may have made countless

mistakes; yet, you are not a mistake. The Word says God knew you before you were formed in your mother's womb, that you were set apart with a purpose to be fulfilled here on earth (Jeremiah 1:5). Jeremiah 29:11 (MSG) is my favorite, where He says: *"I know what I'm doing. I have it all planned out—plans to take care of you, not abandon you, plans to*

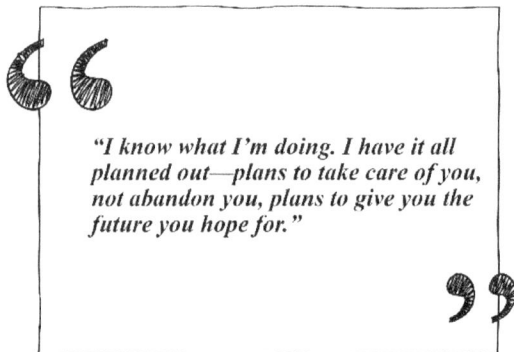

> *"I know what I'm doing. I have it all planned out—plans to take care of you, not abandon you, plans to give you the future you hope for."*

give you the future you hope for."

God knew exactly what He was doing when He designed you, and regardless of the choices you made, that plan is still in effect. He knew the detours you would make, and He allowed it. Remember, we are all "flawed and jacked up" in some way but God is faithful and just to forgive us (2 Corinthians 12:9-10; 1 John 1:9).

BS #2 "God makes everything hard on me; nothing comes to me easy; it is what it is!"

Does this sound like you, the C.E.O woman who, despite beating many odds in your life, you doubt because you've adopted a BS that your life is meant to be "hard?"

Love, maybe you aren't blatantly blaming God, but you can be found touting, "I have had to work hard for everything I have." I too held that BS for a long time and now I call BS on that BS! The problem with this is, I found that it promoted other belief systems that were also BS! It caused me to operate out of a belief that God's love for me was conditional—that His love was based on my performance and if He required that, then so does everyone else. Subsequently, I found myself working "hard" trying to prove my value to my parents, friends, employers, and others. Eventually, working "hard" became a badge of honor once I received validation of my accomplishments. Everything for me became an anticipated uphill battle closing my spirit-mind off to anything coming my way with ease! Are you ready to learn to "Let Go & Let God" in your life? You are not meant to be, as the song says, "climbing up the rough side of the mountain" all the time. It's true that you will have your share of slopes and peaks that lead to mountain top experiences just as you will get to ride the elevator sometimes.

BS#3 "God didn't love me if He let this happen to me."

Does this sound like you, the C.E.O woman who doubts God's love for herself as a result of unimaginable and unexplainable hardships endured in her childhood like abuse, abandonment, or poverty? You may be thinking, "I didn't ask for that to happen to me!" You may be asking, "Why did God allow it?" This BS may be the most difficult to resolve because, as a child, when you are the victim of abuse, neglect, or even poverty, you tend to have overwhelming thoughts and feelings of powerlessness and hopelessness. These thoughts and feelings are also associated with the belief that we are not worthy of love. This was true of my experience as I had many questions surrounding my worth that went unanswered for years.

Child sexual abuse is just one traumatic experience out of many in my life that both changed me and caused me to doubt God's love for me. At first encounter, I was a happy seven-year-old turned victim due to my mom's leaving me in the care of adults she trusted. At that young age, I had a knowledge of God and His love for me because of a vacation Bible school teacher named Mrs. Jones, who introduced me to the Lord. However, the abuse would change my worldview. I started questioning if I was loveable and if anyone could love me. The encounters left me questioning my mere existence. As a result of my work, I know today that it literally changed my brain—that is an impact of trauma. Something inside of me was deeply disturbed, and it would take years to transform the pain I experienced into purpose.

I would be 26 years of age before I realized that the programming from that repeated trauma was still operating in my life. In fact, the trauma was also still a secret I had not told anyone; I mean not a soul! It would be a chain of events that would reveal for me the need to expose the secret but in a strategic way, with a purpose to promote and support healing for myself and my parents. I gathered both my parents, sharing that from the age of 7 to 11, I had been sexually abused. I provided them with as much detail as they required. I even explained to them why I chose to keep it a secret and why I decided to tell them now. I apologized to my father for misappropriating blame towards him as that blame was the root of some of our relationship troubles. Today, we have a loving relationship as he is my loudest cheerleader. Releasing him allowed me to let go of resentment that I was harboring against him and men in general. My parents, though shocked, supported and validated my experience of what I believed, to be the genesis of my healing as an adult from this childhood trauma. Many will travel this road and never receive the human validation that they need to heal, but they are not without healing from the Healer (Psalm 30:2; Psalm 107:20; Proverbs 4:20-22; 1 Peter 2:24).

Let me bring your attention to this one fact. Although I received a supportive response from my parents, I'm yet to confront the perpetrator. I don't need to. I am healed. I haven't received any acknowledgment of the pain caused as a result; I don't need it. I am healed. It has been a personal choice not to expose the perpetrator as I share my story of child sexual abuse as a keynote, conference speaker, and facilitator. It's just one of the ways that I have transformed my pain into purpose in a way that empowers others. I have shared my story with you to support you now; it's your time to dig deep.

Here are your CLAR.R.R.ITY questions:

"What is God doing or wanting to do with you through this?

"What's good about this bad experience, and how can God get the glory out of it?

Or "What's good about this bad experience, and how can I use it to benefit myself or others?"

I shared only three of many faulty belief systems that we C.E.O women have; yet, how do they culminate to answer the question of fulfilling our responsibility to express God's love in the earth?

It is when we choose to accept God's unmerited love for us that we are able to express God's love in the earth. Accepting His love for us means that we accept that we have been forgiven and we are blessed with new mercies daily (Lamentations 3:22-23; NIV). Accepting His love means that we accept that He is **G.O.D – Grace Obtained Daily** and working in our lives (Ephesians 2:4-9). As a result, we can start enjoying a loving relationship with God that others will witness and testify of because it is evident in our lives. Another benefit is that when we embrace how deep, high, and wide God's love is for us personally in our human condition, we then begin to have more love, grace, and compassion on ourselves and others.

I was able to forgive the perpetrator as a child; however, I have had a myriad of opportunities to practice forgiveness with others. I have learned that when you release someone from "what they did to you," you activate that same forgiveness you received. Forgiveness is yet another way I have been able to transform my pain into purpose, thereby allowing me to witness my own transformation. Coincidentally, I didn't just end up forgiving the perpetrator but also myself. As a result, I get to be the witness for many women, men, and children, who are like me—survivors of child sexual abuse who trust me to support them through the pain to a place of purpose.

I share more about my experience on transforming pain into purpose on *The Power Within Podcast with Richale in a series called,* **"Transforming Pain Into Purpose?"** Parts 1 - 3. Listen, share, and let's do this work together because you deserve support. It was never meant for you to journey alone.

Here's how you can ACCESS the Podcast!

The Power Within

Make sure you **Like, Subscribe, & Comment** while there!

Love, what I want you to know is that God takes care to deeply express your significance in the way that He loves you! God's love for you contains the knowledge and wisdom of why you are here, what you will need to fulfill the purpose while you are here, and how and when to supply the deliverables to you.

3
ACT
CHOOSE TO ACT IN FAITH

*"God is not just the author of love but the
author and finisher of our faith!"*

God is not just the author of love but
the author and finisher of our faith (Hebrews
12:2). Over the years, I have witnessed
countless acts of faith in my life and the lives
of others, and I know this to be true.
However, that doesn't always stop fear from
showing up. Would you agree that it is likely
that if faith showed up, the presence of fear
was at the least possible? You have your own
definition of fear that is ingrained in your
psyche. Why? Because at some point in your
childhood, your risk-taking nature was
introduced to it and you learned to be
fearful. What is your first recollection of
being fearful? Take note of that and write it
down. I want you to ponder whether that
same fear still operates in your life today, as
it very well could be. As a result, do you
consistently act in fear or faith?

My spiritual father, Pastor JC Hash Sr.,
is known as a faith teacher and preacher who
teaches faith as a lifestyle. "Faith is a
lifestyle rooted in a trusting relationship with

God. It's a relationship that cannot exist without the acceptance of His love for you and a choice to live inside of His love."

Faith is a lifestyle rooted in a trusting relationship with God. It's a relationship that cannot exist without the acceptance of His love for you and a choice to live inside of His love.

When you embrace the depth of God's love for you, it's easy to trust Him to take the lead and guide you in all truth and righteousness. This is a prerequisite to leading others. Who wants to follow a fearful leader? No one! But in order to get there, you must lead yourself first into becoming fearless. How do you get there? Romans 12 explains your access to faith as a believer, and in verse 3, it shows that God has given every believer "the measure of faith." The measure lets you know that faith can be grown! Just like fear, faith is learned and can be strengthened if you choose to do so. In fact, faith comes by hearing and hearing by the Word of God (Romans 10:17).

CLAR.R.R.ITY question:

"What or who has your ear? Why?"

I love asking this question to my young mogul clients. One young woman I coached, a budding entrepreneur, was experiencing intense anticipatory fear when thinking about the launch of her business and its long-term success. I asked her this question, "What are you feeding your spirit?" She looked puzzled as if she had never heard that question asked before, even though she was a woman of faith. I then said, "I'll know the answer when you share with me your playlist." The look on her face spoke volumes. I was aware that she knew the answer to my question. So, I challenged her in a loving way. I highlighted for her the negative feelings and emotions that she had presented to me in that session before asking her to share with me a song that she might listen to when feeling that emotion. For example, "When you are angry, what song do you listen to?" She named the song, then I asked her to play it for me and the look on her face, again, was so telling. She admitted to literally being ashamed to share the song due to the lyrics. In that instance, her fear of my judgment was voided by her own judgment. I endured the lyrics with her, then asked her if that song "fed into" the feeling of anger for her or not. We repeated this through each emotion she was struggling with, and she realized that through the music, she was feeding the negative emotions that she said she no longer desired. She also realized that she was starving the positive emotions—the ones she desired to have in her life. Does your playlist have the same damaging effect? Take a moment to access your **"Playlist of Emotions"** in your BBTB.

The art of positive emotion management is found in your Emotional Intelligence (EQ). Emotional regulation is your ability to manage your emotions instead of your emotions managing you; the opposite of this is emotional dysregulation. EQ is another benefactor that was not taught in our educational system. Instead, IQ was promoted. Negative emotions can narrow our capacity to think and make wise decisions. When emotionally dysregulated, the major effect of narrowed thinking is a belief that you have no other options. I have coached intellectually sharp women; however, the moment their emotions got in the way, they made poor decisions that impacted their personal and professional growth.

I always tell my clients; *your feelings will trick you*. Have you ever resigned from a position impulsively due to a negative emotion? On a clinical level, this looks like a woman that constantly quits jobs, marriages, and other commitments repeatedly. Or have you ever passed up opportunities for your business to advance because you feared you were not skilled enough to lead? If you knew that your talent was not enough to take you to the next level, would that silence the voice of fear? I agree that fear is a strong emotion that has a loud bolstering voice. As a matter of fact, the thoughts spoken inside your mind process at a speed 3 times more than the rate of the words you speak in one day. If you are thinking negatively, those highly suggestive thoughts are eventually going to come out of your mouth. Those thoughts and confessions shape your reality.

Conversely, positive emotions have the ability to enlarge your capacity to think and make wise decisions. That means that being emotionally regulated impacts your world by suggesting that you have options. If you have been building your "measure of faith," maybe you will even see that you have unlimited possibilities! Now, instead of quitting a job in the heat of the moment, you can make a plan that protects you and those you love through a thought-out decision. Instead of passing yourself up for a promotion, due to fear, you can put faith into play, making a decision to prepare yourself. That's the difference between a conscious decision and a conscious excuse rooted in fear.

Now that you understand that your spirit-mind processes at a faster rate than the words you speak, here are your

CLAR.R.R.ITY questions:

"What would the possibilities look like if your spirit- mind developed the muscle of speaking in faith?"

"Are you challenged by this idea?"

"Why?" "Are you inspired by this idea?"

"To do what?"

I will tell you in short, if you develop the muscle of speaking in faith; eventually, those words are going to overflow out of your mouth in the presence of God. I believe when we speak in faith, it's like beautiful music to God's ear. Secondly, those words are going to overflow out of your mouth in the presence of those you are leading or supporting, thus giving them hope (Matthew 12:34). Speaking words of faith will change your reality and you will begin to materialize what you say (1 Peter 3:10; Proverbs 18:21). Other coaches will tell you that discipline and perseverance are all you need. I agree that while they are necessary muscles, I would consider faith, the milk containing the nutrients the muscles need to grow. What am I saying? Faith is a verb! If you choose to walk in faith, what does faith do?

What Does Faith Do When...

+ **Faith must be FED the Word of God!**

+ **Faith must be STIRRED UP daily!**

= **FAITH FACTS!**

Faith brings **"CLAR.R.R.ITY"** to your situation by operating in the future that you can't see. Let's look at John 8:33, **"Surprised, they said, 'But we're descendants of Abraham. We've never been slaves to anyone. How can you say, 'The truth will free you?'"** Faith also illuminates vision. Being both a woman of faith and a woman of color, this verse illuminates a great deal to me about the condition of our minds as a people. History has constantly told us that we were "slaves," but the truth is, we were "enslaved" to believe that we had no value. This is a condition of the mind that caused the "free slaves" to remain "enslaved." The path was as clear as their choice to take the path. Equally so, it was a choice for those who remained in captivity. What will you choose? It is your continued journey to find the truth of who you are that will free you and allow you to journey from glory to glory. "Richale, what do you mean by glory to glory?" Glory to glory is what we have been talking about all along. It's when the veil is removed, and you "can see and reflect the glory of the Lord. And the Lord—who is the Spirit—makes us more and more like him as we are changed into his glorious image" (2 Corinthians 3:18).

Faith **"SPEAKS"** repeatedly in the Scriptures, reminding you that what you believe you will say (Matthew 17:20; Luke 17:6). Well, what about people who lie and manipulate? Eventually, they slip up. Why? Because what is truly in your heart, you will speak. The words you speak (positive or negative) become your confession and they form your world. I share with my clients in a most colorful way that your confession either produces good juicy fruit or rotten fruit. Once you confess what you believe, the Word also reminds you to stand on your faith. What about the words you are afraid to speak? That is a sign that you may not really believe what you are thinking. What kills faith? Doubt (Mathew 21:21). Lean into the promises of God to avoid this and trust God at His Word. If it is not a lack of faith, maybe you are uncertain about who you share your confession of faith with? I advise that though not everyone can agree with you in faith, find someone who can. I make it a habit to challenge my faith by sharing my statement of faith with someone who I know supports me. When I say challenge my faith, I don't mean to infer that you can achieve or receive more faith. It's simply to stir it up and your awareness is increased. The truth sometimes is that the same person may not have enough faith to believe for themselves, but they admire you for your faith and support you. Also, they may need to grow in their faith as a result of witnessing you. There is someone you can trust who shares genuine excitement for you as you believe God to meet you at the point of your need, want, or desire. Overall, remember that God is the author and finisher of your faith (Hebrews 12:2).

Let me share with you one more thing that will kill faith that many people miss. In one word, "sin" kills faith at the root! With a sin consciousness, you will not be able to speak boldly in faith with any positive results. In our society, we tend to place judgment and degree on what is "right" or "wrong." As a result, we overlook crucial elements that spoil relationships. Your relationship with God has everything to do with how you treat and speak to others. If you are going to go boldly to God for anything, you need to make sure that your lifestyle truly exemplifies His. You expect God to keep His Word, don't you? Of course! Well then, in the same fashion, are you a woman of your Word? Can God trust you to represent Him in the marketplace that your word is your bond? In order to go to God boldly, you must live right with all people. Be a woman of your word. If you say you are going to do something, do it! If you cannot do it, go to that person and talk it out. Don't have them looking for you to figure out what happened. C.E.O women represent God by keeping their word and living a life inside of Christ that will make others want to do the same. Isn't that exciting, that as I walk upright before God, others might be inspired to know Him too? People are watching your faith walk, what will it speak to them?

Faith, when spoken, **OVERCOMES"** adversity through your relationship with Christ (Revelation 12:11; 1 John 1:5)! Do you desire to be an overcomer? Then feed that desire! When you have overcoming faith, you are like a storm chaser. Not that you are looking for adversity, but when it shows up, you don't fear it because faith confronts fear (Matthew 6:33). Instead, you will look for opportunities in the storm? You simply see that storm as new unchartered territory, and your faith cultivates the environment of expectation. You may not know how you are going to get through; you just believe with God's help, you will. Instead of following the crowd, your head is above the crowd looking for the opportunity. You are not moved by what you see but that faith you have been feeding on is what gives you direction. You are not moved by the faces of those around you nor do you fear what they might do to you (Hebrews 13:5-6). That's the sign of a bona fide C.E.O woman, first leading herself, then others. Your heart and mind are fixed and you have peace in a faithful God (Isaiah 26:2-3). When you have overcoming faith, you will be able to make your decisions in peace (John 16:33). Faithful C.E.O women learn that in adversity, they don't have to operate from a state of panic, chaos, and reactivity. "For the faithful C.E.O, faith is your first response and you will know it because you choose to speak in faith!"

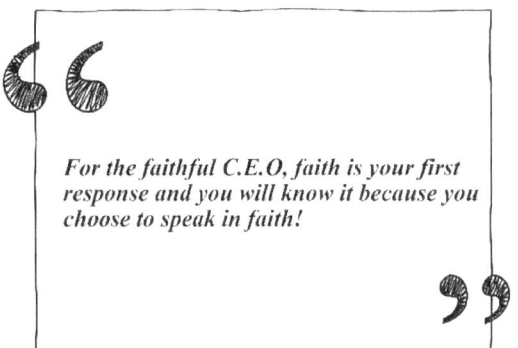

For the faithful C.E.O, faith is your first response and you will know it because you choose to speak in faith!

Faith **"ADVOCATES"** on your behalf, giving you the winning advantage! For example, you may be saying, "Richale, I don't have any support; so, what do I do?" I understand you may be rebuilding a healthy support network by making yourself open to it. In that case, God is all you need in the first place. Still, make your confession known to God. When you speak in faith, you keep your mind and thoughts in the atmosphere of faith where God can work on your behalf. Research shows that faithful women have increased overall physical and mental health with spiritual well-being. There's a direct correlation to increased resilience as a result. Remember, faith is a muscle we are building and all muscles have muscle memory. Your mind has muscle memory. When a woman falls while exercising the muscle of resilience, and she is rooted in faith, it quickly picks her back up!

When you are making your confessions known to God, I advise writing down what you are believing Him for, so that you can keep a physical and mental record which will build your faith immensely as you go back years later to see what you have transformed in your life with His guidance. Journal about the outcome as well to retain the thoughts, feelings, and emotions around it, including other pertinent details. For example, you may even include how your request was answered with a "NO!" Oh yes, God answers but sometimes, the answer is, "NO!" Faith prepares you for this and other challenges. You may need more time to get CLAR.R.R.ITY on that but it will come. Remember, even the "NOs" work together for your good (Romans 8:28).

I know that your faith has been fed! I know your faith has been stirred up! What I don't know is what action will your faith take now? Faith is a verb! Faith does not

72

make excuses…faith is now. Now, choose faith! You can access your CLAR.R.R.ITY questions and mind-shift exercise **"From Forecast to Futurecast"** in your **BBTB.**

4

THE TRIPLE R EFFECT
REVEAL, RENEW, REIGNITE

"Healing in the presence of Christ will reveal, renew, reignite your life, and transform it."

Sister C.E.O, I have shared with you a mere snippet of the pain that I have transformed. Some of that pain was rooted in my childhood, and because I internalized them for years, I suffered unnecessarily. However, it's not always that those infractions and downright violations are rooted in our childhood. Sometimes, they are old infractions that seem as fresh as last week; old infractions that are still ongoing as of last week, or new ones that actually happened last week. As faithful women, we have internalized a host of problems. We are adults with "mommy or daddy issues," "church hurt," body image issues, control issues, relationship issues with food, sex, men or women, and people in authority, and the list goes on. As adult women, we also experience social injustices such as discrimination, ageism, racism, and unfair treatment in the workplace, thereby creating additional challenges to remember our spiritual nature. You may have felt alone in your struggle, but you are not alone as there is not a woman living who has not been bruised, scarred, and deeply wounded in some way. Despite that commonality, you are the only one who can do the work of healing. I have done my work and I want to support you in yours. As your coach, I am here to honor your journey which means if you are not ready, I cannot force you to be. It also means that as much as I want forward traction for you, I cannot do it for you. It is by your faith that you are made whole (Luke 4:23 and Mark 5:34).

Reveal, Renew, and Reignite is a three-step process of renewing your mind in Christ. It is based on Romans 12:2: **"And be not conformed to this world: but be ye transformed by the renewing of your mind, that ye may prove what is that good, and acceptable, and perfect, will of God."** The truth is that your mind can actually undergo a process of transformation, renewal, and rejuvenation the moment you give it permission. Research in neuroscience suggests that your brain has a reset point. Your choice determines your ability to see yourself as you really are; the end result is CLAR.R.R.ITY because you were willing to look into the mirror of God's Word and see yourself for who you really are (2 Cor 3:18). A keynote throughout this process is that you must see yourself accepting of the ideas presented which will promote your brain operating in harmony with what you imagine and speak in the authority of God's word.

*This process is not intended for deep-seated clinical issues without the support of a licensed professional. Please, contact a Christian counselor or therapist to help you transform.** To learn more about therapy and coaching join me on The Power Within Podcast with Richale, "The Difference Between Counseling & Coaching" Episode #9.

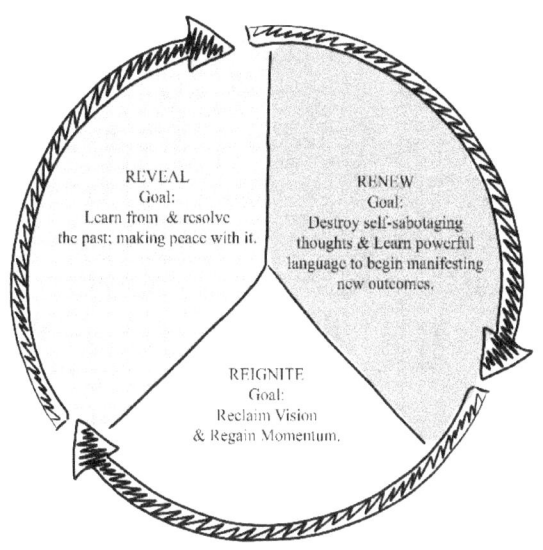

REVEAL
Goal:
Learn from & resolve
the past; making peace with it.

RENEW
Goal:
Destroy self-sabotaging
thoughts & Learn powerful
language to begin manifesting
new outcomes.

REIGNITE
Goal:
Reclaim Vision
& Regain Momentum.

PHASE 1: REVEAL – YOU CAN'T ADDRESS SOMETHING YOU WON'T CALL OUT

In the **REVEAL** phase, you choose to reveal the sabotaging thoughts, feelings, or emotions we will call "pain points" in three categories of your life: personally, professionally, and spiritually. This is the start point where you "sit with" your thoughts, feelings, and emotions, and you tell yourself the truth about it. This is where you "call a thing a thing." It is integral in this phase that you name "it." For example, I have clients who may admit that "mom's beatings berated me daily" but have difficulty saying "it was abusive" or "I was abused by my mom." What is eating at you? Go through this process for every area you uncover within the three categories. Ensure you take your time to fully process your thoughts through the three domains. Once those pain points are identified, ask yourself these powerful *CLAR.R.R.ITY questions:*

> *What threatens or pains me about this? Be specific.*
>
> *In what ways has this negatively impacted my life?*
>
> *What activity/event/persons trigger negative thoughts, feelings, or emotions?*
>
> *What would a faithful woman do in a situation like mine?*

The goals here are many: learn from the past, resolve it, and begin the process of making peace with it. Validate your experience by telling the truth about it and its impact on you. Becoming clear on what you can control and what you cannot is what we get to do. We do not get to control others. As a result, you'll begin to increase in awareness about what is holding you back. See Proverbs 29:18.

PHASE 2: RENEW – THE PROCESS OF RENEWING YOUR MIND WITH GODLY RATIONALE THAT PROMOTES INPOWERMENT

In the **RENEW** phase, you replace the negative thoughts or fears with not merely positive self-talk, but with the Word of God. As a result of being created in Christ, you have power over these thoughts and can "cast them down." In other words, you can challenge them (2 Corinthians 10:5). The key distinction here is that we are not getting rid of, covering up, or numbing, but we are replacing it with the Word of God (the mind of Christ) which is power to the faithful woman C.E.O (1 Corinthians 2:13-16). Instead of getting rid of, you are still in the process of sitting with "the issue and honoring it through acceptance." In this stage, you realize that "it" does not define you, so you can remove the power you have allowed it to have over you. In this phase, you are restoring to a fresh state through the renewing of the mind. This the fruit-producing stage that comes as a result of doing your work. Our power is in when we access mind renewal and intentional choices that please God as a result of seeking and searching the mind of God continually (Romans 12:2; Mathew 7:7-8). When you renew your mind, you renew the whole woman. Here are your ***CLAR.R.R.ITY questions***:

> ***What does the Word say about it?***
>
> ***What new thinking (perspective) do I have?***
>
> ***What new opportunities do I have?***
>
> ***What does God want me to learn from this?***

The goal here is to destroy self-sabotaging thoughts and begin manifesting what you desire through confessing the Word of God over your life. It's a confession of faith; the faithful C.E.O's way of affirming self. Additionally, you'll cultivate an atmosphere that promotes new thinking, a sound mind, and a renewed spirit (Psalm 51:10). This is where you sustain a change in your spirit-mind, gaining a new heart (clean), a new spirit (right), new mercies, enlightenment, a surrendered will, softened conscience, and rectified thoughts. This is where you get revelation.

PHASE 3: REIGNITE – THE PROCESS OF STANDING IN FAITH & FLAMING HOPE

In the Reignite phase, you give new life or energy to your goals, dreams, and desires. It is where you stand in faith, knowing that you have stood in your faith well (2 Timothy 4:7). In this phase, you will begin the journey of making peace with that past, allowing for forwarding traction needed for successful coaching. Write down what you are believing God for and when you feel as if you can't stand any longer marinate on Ephesians 6:13 (MSG):

"Be prepared. You're up against far more than you can handle on your own. Take all the help you can get, every weapon God has issued, so that when it's all over but the shouting you'll still be on your feet. Truth, righteousness, peace, faith, and salvation are more than words. Learn how to apply them. You'll need them throughout your life. God's Word is an indispensable weapon. In the same way, prayer is essential in this ongoing warfare. Pray hard and

long. Pray for your brothers and sisters. Keep your eyes open. Keep each other's spirits up so that no one falls behind or drops out."

Remain prayerful! Read these additional verses and meditate on them in this phase: Luke 1:37; Mark 11:24; Proverbs 3:5-6, & Mark 9:23. Your CLAR.R.R.ITY questions and mind-shift exercise **"Reveal, Renew, Reignite"** can be found in your BBTB. I did a powerful series on this on my podcast, *The Power Within Podcast with Richale. Listen to the entire series on "Reflection," ending with special attention to episode #33 **Reflection: Reveal, Renew, Reignite"** for more CLAR.R.RITY on the Triple R Effect.*

5

IAMNESS
CHOOSE TO WALK IN DIVINE
PURPOSE & VISION

"It has been said that the two most important days in a person's life are the day on which she was born, and the day on which she discovers why she was born." Ernest T. Campbell

I've long recognized a love for and a joy of observing butterflies. I am intrigued by their still beauty sitting on a rock, flower, or me. I am more intrigued by their uniqueness and symphony of motion in flight. A few years ago, I rediscovered an old photo of myself when I was brought home from the hospital. I had seen this photo many times; now I realize that I saw, but I didn't see. Has that ever happened to you? ***Many times, as the chief executive officer of our own lives, we see but don't see; we see but don't understand what we see, and we see but with limited or no vision.*** This is dangerous because without a vision, peril is inevitable, as purpose is not achieved (Proverbs 29:18).

I was going through a difficult time when this realization blessed me to see the butterfly bedsheets I was laying on while I slept peacefully. I then realized that many of the businesses that I had throughout the years were branded in one way or another after a characteristic of the butterfly. And yet today, it will not escape me, that this might be the reason this work is titled with the same intention. It's that natural fit that if I migrate from, would feel inauthentic for me and disturb what I now know as a part of the whole of my "IAMNESS." *You see, simply put, your IAMNESS is your awareness of whose you are and who you are, with a clear connection to what you do.*

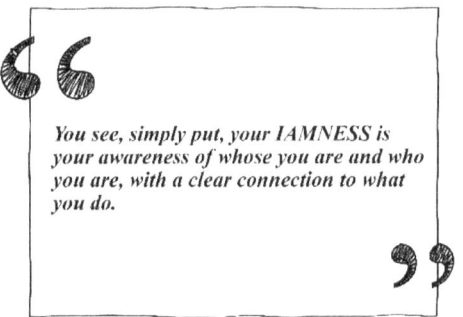

You see, simply put, your IAMNESS is your awareness of whose you are and who you are, with a clear connection to what you do.

It may seem backward, but I want to share with you what you do before we explore whose and who you are. Make sure you are ready to take notes, while I coach you through this thought process. Take a moment to consider what you are really good at doing. There is a successful coach I know who brands herself with this quote which serves as your ***CLAR.R.R.ITY question:***

"I may suck at a lot of things but ___ ain't one of them."

You are not confessing that you suck at anything, but I know you have heard that before. I need you to go ahead and laugh, not taking yourself so seriously, and fill in the blank with your answer. There is a vision that leads to a wealth of understanding in this answer. Now, if you are multitalented, complete that sentence as many times as you need to before moving on.

Next CLAR.R.R.ITY question:

"In what ways is my gift showing up in my life?"

If you cannot answer that question well, choose not to beat yourself up. The question, like all the other CLAR.R.R.ITY questions, is diagnostic. "What do you mean, Richale?" I mean that it explains your current level of awareness regarding your giftedness and lets you and I know where we <u>are</u> as opposed to where we want to go. This question is just one in the line of questions that promote a way forward, thus increasing CLAR.R.R.ITY in your life. So, why is it essential to operate from areas of giftedness?

85

Proverbs 18:16 (NKJV) is a powerful statement that reveals the answer: *"A woman's gift makes room for her."* It is in exercising this gift that you will find real fulfillment, purpose, and contentment in your work. Your gift is clearly designed to create a space for you in this world; to make a way for you in life. The result is a life filled with purpose and vision to be fulfilled. It allows you to fine-tune every decision you make to the point that anything outside of it, is an easy, "NO!' Why? Because there is no room for it. Your gift lets you know how to answer the call; that is, the call on your life. It's your spiritual caller ID which will make your "YES" your "YES!" and your "NO" your "NO!" Your gift is a spiritual alignment to your boundaries and processes, giving you the much-needed structure required for destiny.

A gift is a gift. It's God-given; you don't have to work for it. However, you are required to perfect it, i.e., work on it. Essentially, your gift works for you! Stop at nothing to discover your gifts because that is where your provision lies. You must do the work to discover why you were created, but do it with a knowing that a specific purpose and plan are available for you. Pursue it in faith with this promise in Jeremiah 29:10-11(MSG):

This is GOD's Word on the subject: "As soon as Babylon's seventy years are up and not a day before, I'll show up and take care of you as I promised and bring you back home. I know what I'm doing. I have it all planned out—plans to take care of you, not abandon you, plans to give you the future you hope for.

Just in case you missed that, here is my translation; in the R.R.R version, God is saying,

"I know you've been through Hell and back! You didn't die. I didn't allow it! It's all purposeful and planned. You have not been abandoned; you have been hidden and set apart for a time that I will bring you to. You may think you have gone down the wrong road, made a bad decision, I allowed that too! Stop trippin'; I got you!"

> *I know you've been through Hell and back! You didn't die. I didn't allow it! It's all purposeful and planned. You have not been abandoned; you have been hidden and set apart for a time that I will bring you to. You may think you have gone down the wrong road, made a bad decision, I allowed that too! Stop trippin'; I got you!"*

I don't know about you, but that is how I read the Scriptures, how I hear His voice, and how I flow when I go to Him in prayer. A personal relationship with Him will do that for you; it will liberate you from God being the God of your parents, grandparents, and so on, to being the God of your understanding. I have worked with many clients who I had to be honest with, saying, "You treat God like He is your distant cousin, twice removed, instead of intimately like your Heavenly Father." It changes the game for them for an outsider to see that and call it out. It's like God is "a god" in your life. No, He wants to be the "GOD" of and in your life. God is your God, and He is the One who created you. He knows all about you and gave you His name (Romans 8:15). I have learned to be naked and unashamed before Him. I have learned to take my pain before Him and heal before Him because He cares.

See, He is very aware of what you have accomplished despite it all. He expected nothing less; you are, His. I say this with love: He is not concerned about your degrees, titles, and awards, but the condition of your mind and heart (Matthew 5:8). He wants you to know who and whose you are (2 Corinthians 5:21). He wants you to walk in "IAMNESS" so you can fulfill your calling (John 1:34).

Consequently, when you don't use your gifts, you find yourself in a room that you simply don't fit in, frustrated, confused, void of passion, joy, and vision to fulfill your purpose. Now, we left off with the CLAR.R.R.ITY question, "How is my gift showing up in my life?" If you couldn't answer that affirmatively and with confidence, then here is your next **CLAR.R.R.ITY question, "How would my life change if I stepped into the current of my gifting?"**

Is the reason your gift is not activated because you have it attached to the thought that you or the gift sucks? Really, do you doubt the Creator's assignment of the gift He gave you? If so, you operate out of insufficiency, scarcity, and lack with that thinking, which is a hindrance. What about humility? Do you think it's an act of humility to minimize and downplay your gifting; showing up small? This is not an act of humility; God needs you to show up and show out. He needs your "IAMNESS" on display (Matthew 5:14). Will you selflessly give your gift away to the world? It's not as overwhelming as it sounds. "The world" is simply those that He will assign you to help.

Now think, if you are multitalented, how do your gifts complement each other? Let's look at this in a 360- degree view by adding the perceived difficulties that the transition might bring your way, including the resolutions to those difficulties, while still focusing on the overarching benefits of that transition. This process will help you to identify the limiting beliefs you have, allowing you to challenge them before shifting your focus to the "YES" that is needed in your spirit to move forward. When you move forward, others will testify of who you are, confirming for you what you know in your heart.

Remember my connection to the butterfly? I myself, I'm so skilled at what I do now, that others testify to my IAMNESS" by referring to me as a "change-agent" and one who brings "clarity" to their lives; hence, the C.LAR.R.R.ITY Coach." It's not forced; it just is because my essence exudes "IAMNESS." On a simpler note, it is the reason that I am drawn to and known for wearing butterfly shades! Hear me, there was a time when I was unaware of the connection. All I knew is that I was drawn to any and everything butterfly. However, now it has become my intentional brand. **What I've discovered is when you pay attention, you can begin to apply intention, creating the life that was destined for you.** That's CLAR.R.R.ITY! You'll lose yourself in that space because walking in "IAMNESS" through your work becomes both sacred and necessary for you. It's what gives you life!

Now, what is really liberating is when you realize that this really doesn't have to make sense to anyone but you. So many times, you find yourself fighting for others to understand you when all that is necessary is that you speak your truth through the way you live, work, and play so that others can witness and make their own decision;

hopefully, to respect yours. That means you spend less time in a negative space trying to convince others of what you chose for your life. You can now agree to disagree because all you are responsible for is the life you were gifted to manage.

I believe there is a calling to INpowerment in our lives as C.E.O women conquering everyday obstacles. The calling is to live IN power; over our spirit minds. I've shared with you how the butterfly is a symbol that resonates with me and INpowers me, reminding me to stay true to living my life from the inside out. I want to share that same experience with you, so stop here and access your BBTB for your mind-shift exercise. The *"INpowerment Symbol"* was designed to get your creative juices flowing, anchor you, and INpower you. Be sure to bookmark this location.

I know you enjoyed creating your symbol. My INpowerment symbol has been with me since childhood and was a comfort, even when I didn't realize it, as I went through Hell. As a licensed therapist, I teach those I care for that in order to move forward; you have to be intentional about revisiting the past to promote healing in a safe way. Also, as a therapist, I am not immune to having to revisit my past to evoke healing, as I shared with you in Chapter 2. Maybe you are like me, perhaps you had a traumatic childhood, but now realize there's been a hedge of protection over you because you've been through Hell and back, and you are still here. Let's do some workaround through a mind-shift exercise. Life is requiring you to visit it now to continue the healing process so that you can come into your "IAMNESS" with boldness. This next mind-shift exercise will take you some time before you move on. Please, make sure you have dedicated space and time to give to it. Use your empowerment symbol as your anchor and a Scripture that reminds you of your "IAMNESS" and that you are safe now. It's time to access your BBTB for your mind-shift exercise, **"Unpacking My Suitcase."**

So, now that you have unpacked your suitcase, you feel lighter, right? Great. Now, I need you to get your tool belt and put it back on. There are a few more tools you are going to need for the journey. Read Ephesians 6:11-18.

6

TOOLS

CHOOSE TOOLS OF TRANSFORMATION

"Vulnerability allows you to witness your authentic beauty; transparency invites others to witness it."

Despite the not-so convincing backdrop from early childhood through adulthood, I've always held a strong belief that my life had a purpose. Growing up impoverished was my first recollection of what it means to suffer. Inopportunely, I know I was not alone in this. Even today, approximately 15 million children in the United States are officially poor, according to a 2019 report from the National Center for Children In Poverty. Even more alarming is UNICEF's reporting that 663 million children worldwide are impoverished and most countries have yet to prioritize the epidemic. Poverty is a devastating condition having wide- range effects on the physical, mental health, and overall well- being of children. Its effects can last long into adulthood. Don't get me wrong, like many others with my same backdrop, though impoverished; we made the best of what we had. My mother made sure of that; she was conquering everyday obstacles and showing me the way.

Christmas came for me twice a year—that was at the start of every new school year and tax time! Every year before the start of school, and again at tax time, I could not wait to go clothes-shopping with her at my favorite store affectionately named, "Potato Chips" in downtown Elizabeth, New Jersey. She had a budget and a method all her own. I love sharing this story every chance I get a microphone. My mom was the master of coordinating five pairs of pants with five shirts to make it appear as if I had a larger wardrobe than I did. I loved watching her work her magic. Though money was tight, in my mom's opinion, there was no reason to look like it. She taught me how to take care of those clothes too. To this day, anyone who knows me will tell you I take great care of everything I am blessed with.

Although not all my memories were as pleasant as the former, they are not without significance. A memory that almost always brings a tear to my eye is that of my mother going without eating so that my sister and I would have enough to eat. She was a diligent worker, never heard complaining about not having enough. She just prepared the food and watched us eat. At the time, I was too young to realize the impact of her sacrifice, nor was I old enough to understand the impact of poverty on suffering. Hindsight, she actually made sacrificing look easy. And little did I know that these experiences and others would significantly shape the rest of my life.

As you have heard, my early childhood and adolescent years were riddled with trauma. I would suffer, yet in silence, for nearly four years as a victim of child sexual abuse. I'd endure bullying by two of the meanest girls in Linden, New Jersey, whose faces today I can still see clearly, and their names (first and last), I can recall. At around eleven to twelve years old, as if things could get any worse, I would spend months trying to convince the adults in my life that my mother was not "herself" and needed help. Nearly six months had passed before she was hospitalized, and my world essentially turned upside down. Everything from that point on would be unfamiliar, uncomfortable, and undesired changes in my life. I'd soon realize I was earning an advanced degree in suffering when my mother and I were shipped, about six or so months later, to Winston-Salem, North Carolina. My first lesson, "I was a damned Yankee!" My second lesson, "'Yankees' were not wanted in 'them thar parts!'"

Fast-forwarding to, "Get me out of here!" I so wanted to leave badly, but I was "stuck!" Apparently, I overstayed my welcome having been there long enough to become a victim again. And it would take years to "call a thing a thing." The state of shock was temporary; however, the state of denial lasted for years before finally giving voice to the truth that I had been a victim of date rape which resulted in my pregnancy. I would now make a decision that went against my very conscience and faith—I chose to have an abortion. Not at all an easy decision; I could not have fathomed that this would be the most dehumanizing decision of my life. Who had I become? I honestly did not know and that became evident in my life for some time to come as I made foolish decisions as a result of my pain. Although I told my immediate family, I didn't speak on it for years to anyone else unless it was necessary to help them in their decision.

I remember the first time I was led to share my story with a young lady I was getting to know. I thought about every negative scenario that could result from my sharing, but the primary thought was, "What if she exposed me?" "What if she went to church and told our acquaintances?" "What would I do?" I battled with these thoughts but not for long because I realized that none of that mattered. What was done was done! My sacrifice was my pride, my reputation, my comfort, and my ego! And as I write, my ego is thinking, "And now you are going to broadcast that experience and memorialize it in this book?" Essentially, another decision that I will have to live with for the rest of my life once I hit "publish." And I will hit "publish," choosing to continue living my life in a way that liberates me to live inside of God's love for me. I will hit "publish," freeing myself from my own judgment as well as that of others. I will hit "publish" because I am not afraid to walk in my truth, not yours. My truth! I will hit "publish" because my life is not mine. I will hit "publish" because my reputation, comfort, and ego are unimportant to God. I will hit "publish" because some woman needs to, not just hear my story, but hear how with God's help, I overcame (Philippians 2:3).

I believe the immense suffering I endured prepared me for being uncomfortable. In my experience, there is nothing much more uncomfortable than "sitting with" yourself and telling yourself the truth. "I figured out that as I was willing to do my life's work wrapped in the arms of a loving God, He would hide, cover, and protect me, then use me for His glory. I realized that as I was willing to do my life's work, God would fulfill lifework through me."

> *I figured out that as I was willing to do my life's work wrapped in the arms of a loving God, He would hide, cover, and protect me, then use me for His glory. I realized that as I was willing to do my life's work, God would fulfill lifework through me.*

Sister C.E.O, if you are seeking CLAR.R.R.ITY that leads to a transformed life, I recommend the tools of vulnerability, transparency, and authenticity. It has been the tools of vulnerability and transparency that allow me to wield the tool of being authentically and unapologetically me. I believe that vulnerability allows you to witness your authentic beauty, while transparency invites others to witness it likewise. It was through the eyes and in the arms of God that I first felt safe enough to be both vulnerable and transparent, eventually allowing me to walk in authenticity. This is the result of the process of inncr work. This is life inside of Christ. Today, vulnerability allows me to risk living in my truth in the face of God and others. Transparency allows me to promote the truth about my experience to God, myself, and others.
Authenticity allows me to just be me. Most

INpowering, is that when you choose to go there, you choose to connect authentically with all those God created you to touch. My question is, "Who does God need you to touch?" Someone needs to hear it and how you have overcome. I have shared my story of overcoming with you but "What's your story of overcoming?" and "How will you share it?"

I began to intentionally use writing as a conduit for my healing later in life. The writings began in private, and as a matter of fact, that is how my first book was written— *Silhouette of Her Naked & Unashamed: A Poetic Journey of Faith.* I had no idea it was a book when I began. I was just writing about the process of overcoming pain when I felt led to compile the poems and then create *A Letter of Love from Richale* that would accompany each poem. I discovered that writing allowed me to process my thoughts, feelings, and emotions while privately ushering in my healing. I enjoy taking my clients through all types of mind-shift exercises that involve writing. You were created to create, and writing is one of the most creative processes you can enter that leads you to more CLAR.R.R.ITY, and so I have created **"Authentic Journaling Prompts"** for you in your BBTB. The prompts are designed to both challenge and develop your ability to be vulnerable, transparent, and authentic with yourself and God first. The prompts are designed to also promote your continued healing and you will know when it's time to share your story. Additional support is available by listening to episode 5-6, **"What's Your Story?"** and **"Heal Thyself,"** episode 4, on *The Power Within Podcast with Richale*.

Sister C.E.O, it is most important that you heal because others are attached to your healing. However, healing is work you must agree to for a greater purpose than what you can see right now. Will you allow yourself to heal? Allowing yourself this time guarantees massive impact beyond what you imagine. Will you take your pain before Him and heal in His presence so you can live without the mask? He cares. God wants to alleviate the pressure of wearing the mask because He cares so much for you (1 Peter 5:7). Someone needs to hear your story of healing and how you have overcome to encourage theirs. I would love to hear your story of healing and overcoming.

Again, if you believe you need more support in healing, contact a loving faith-based counselor licensed in your state of residence. If you need support with thinking into your future possibilities consider a *certified* coach anywhere in the world. Coaching is an investment in you and you are worthy of support.

7
YIELD
CHOOSE TO YIELD TO THE PROCESS

Have Thine own way, Lord!
Have Thine own way!
Thou art the Potter, I am the clay.
Mold me and make me after Thy will;
While I am waiting, yielded and still.

Adelaide A. Pollard 1902

Finally, you are coming to an end, not *the* end. You have journeyed with this Black Butterfly doing your work and now it's time that you understand what it means to be yielded and still. You might think quite naturally that it means to be still, but it means more than that. You have actually been in the process and now you have your wings…butterfly wings…you can now take flight. But what does that look like for you?

Naturally a high energetic person, extremely driven, and passionate in my younger years, I have always found it difficult to rest my body and mind. I viewed others who were constantly found resting in a negative light until I met my husband. Years into our marriage, I realized that God was trying to teach me how to rest through Him. I remember challenging myself to rest the same way he did, and it was really uncomfortable. I couldn't understand how he could do it for an entire weekend. One weekend, I shared with him my frustration with myself when he gently said to me, "Babe, you have to find out what rest looks like for you." He further explained, "Rest for you is not sitting doing nothing." He was right; I saw that as a waste of time. He reminded me, "You are always grinding, but think about it, even God rested on the seventh day." I realized that this is essentially a rest of my spirit.

The truth was, I had programmed my mind and body to perform under high stress for extended periods of time with little time to recuperate in my early days. Although still highly driven and passionate, my husband reminded me that I was getting older and my body, mind, *and spirit* could not perform on the same level under those conditions, especially when my eating is not on point. However, God is not through with me yet; I am just getting started, so there has to be a solution beyond my human limitations, I thought. That's right, I am a spiritual being having a human experience, and it's not to take priority over my spiritual nature. I have been looking at it from a disadvantaged perspective; it is life in the spirit that gives me the advantage. Now that I was seeking, God was opening my eyes through the lives of my clients. Their ability to be vulnerable allowed me to become very clear on what unrest looked like, the dangers of it, and why a spirit-mind shift is vital.

What I observed were extreme cases of women who were constantly busy doing nothing. They were worried about everything, anxious due to the constant state of "high alert," highly reactive, always in crisis mode, stressed out, problem- focused, distracted, as well as overwhelmed with and exhausted from their work. This is what life outside of Christ looks like. Clearly, there is no benefit in this. In fact, it's quite damaging to our physical, mental health, and spiritual well- being. And is God getting any glory out of this? So, where do you need to make a shift? I share this quote by Zig Ziglar with my clients all the time, *"You are either a wandering generality or a meaningful specific."*

"You are either a wandering generality or a meaningful specific."

The quote reminds me that there is such a thing as "meaningful and specific work." However, John 6:25-29 (NIV) tells me what "meaningful specific work" is for the faithful woman conquering everyday obstacles:

"Jesus answered, 'Very truly I tell you, you are looking for me, not because you saw the signs I performed but because you ate the loaves and had your fill. Do not work for food that spoils, but for food that endures to eternal life, which the Son of Man will give you. For on him God the Father has placed his seal of approval.' Then they asked him, 'What must we do to do the works God requires?" Jesus answered, 'The work of God is this: to believe in the one he has sent.'"

What we have here is the meaning of

"meaningful and specific work" for the faithful woman C.E.O. Essentially, regardless of your profession, if you confess that you believe, then your work is the same as mine; that is the work of God which is "to believe in the one he has sent" (John 6:29). How you express that belief in the world may vary in *form*, but the *essence* is the same. The question becomes, **"How will you serve God?"** My point is the one that I have proposed throughout this book; that is, God needs you and me to express His love for us on the earth. We are ineffective when we simply do the "good things" instead of the "God things;" *that is,* the work He has called us specifically to.

Furthermore, if we are to do "meaningful and specific work," then we must even be intentional about resting. We must rest on purpose with purpose. Hebrews 4:9-11 says, "So then, there remains a Sabbath rest for the people of God, for whoever has entered God's rest has also rested from his work as God did from his. Let us therefore strive to enter that rest…" When we rest "in" God, we rest inside of the relationship and the partnership we have with God. He is the Source of our work and the Source of our supply

(Philippians 4:19).

Remember, in Chapter 1, I shared the confession, "In Christ I live, move, and have my being?" I said that I needed you to catch that and hold onto it without letting go because once you choose to live life inside of Christ, you choose to SURRENDER to LIVING, DOING, and BEING ALL in your own strength! Do you want to transform your life? Live a life YIELDED and STILL before God.

What might yielding look like for those of us who have struggled in this area? I'll tell you; it looks like practical exercises with spiritual impact. These exercises are unique to you and your needs. I've compiled a list of exercises to feed your spirit. Your complete checklist, **"Yielded & Still"** is in your BBTB.

- o Do anything different from your normal "work."
- o Pray; meditate with or without music
- o Reflect quietly with or without writing
- o Keep a song in your heart; hum, sing worship, or praise
- o Breathing exercises
- o Laugh with intention
- o Draw or creatively write

- Express gratitude (verbally or written form)
- Think on where God has brought you from
- Plan your next move for God while sitting in the park Listen to calming, instrumental, classical, or worship music
- Get some sleep or rest longer, increasing the time periodically
- Take a hot shower
- Get a massage
- Take time to caress your own body
- Spend time doing something you enjoy (hobby)
- Read the Word of God

What are the benefits of resting "in meaningful and specific work?" When we

YIELDED & STILL	
Benefits of Resting on Meaningful Work	
Outside of Christ	Inside of Christ
Good Work	God work
Busy/Unproductive	Fruit Bearing
Panicked	Purposeful
Fearful	Faithful
Disconnected & Uninspired	Connected to Source & Genius
Anxious	Expecting Great Things
Destination Focused	Journey-Focused
Problem-Focused	Solution-Focused
Double-minded	

are engaged in meaningful work, we are connected to God; we are living inside of Christ. We are inspired, passionate, and compassionate. We have a reason to rise and shine. I always say, if you are going to rise, you might as well shine. Meaningful and specific work brings you CLAR.R.R.ITY of purpose in a life in Christ.

Don't forget to access your BBTB for your YIELDED & STILL" graphic using the QR code located on page 12.

These are just some ways to reconnect to the Source and some of the benefits of the inner life in Christ I have seen in my life and the lives of my clients. I learned that if I were going to rest in Christ, I had to allow it. I had to consider what limited thinking was costing and denying me, even what I knew I needed. Resting gives you the power that you need to engage in the meaningful and specific work you were purposed for. Resting is a matter of honoring your Creator, self, and those you are called to serve.

FINAL WORDS

The name of this work, *A Black Butterfly's Journey Towards CLAR.R.R.ITY Reveal, Renew, Reignite,* was given to me by my SOURCE and supply, God. The name, like everything else He gives me, signifies not just change but the process of transformation. Interestingly enough, but not surprising to me, as I began to create this body of work, I started an intensive deep-dive in my life where I needed more CLAR.R.R.ITY. I believe it was necessary to not only grow me but to support you in your growth as well. I have come to know this one thing for sure that our lives are not our own.

Over the years, I have been blessed to witness women like yourself as you transform. As a witness, there is indeed a pain that is experienced with the propensity for grief to set in. However, because as I witness, I do so with great expectancy of your increased knowledge of Christ in you, who is the hope of glory. My expectancy serves as an all- consuming fire, leaving nothing left but joy in my heart for you. Thank you for allowing me to share His love with you today. I see it as my responsibility to share His love in a way that brings increased self-love, self-respect, and confidence to courageous women like yourself.

We live in a society that has controlled our thinking about who we are, what we can be, and the impact we can make in our lives and the lives of others. Group thinking has limited our limitless possibilities by corrupting the way we perceive ourselves, family, culture, faith, and money. Though this is the truth as I see it, and there is plenty of evidence to support it, we have a responsibility not only to ourselves but to those we are called to serve through our leadership. We were birthed as servants one to another, not lovers of ourselves (2 Timothy 3:1-2). Remember, our lives are not our own! I believe through your leadership in your own life first, like me, we can transform our individual and corporate experience; we _can_ change the world.

I pray that you now have crystal clear CLAR.R.R.ITY on how bright your future is as a result of deciding to go through the birthing process, and choosing to do the work of gifting yourself to the world. It is the

transformed woman who welcomes a
renewal of the mind, body, and spirit as she
embraces challenges that she expects to
overcome because of the Greater one who
lives on the inside (1 John 1-5).

Photo by: Christina C. Williams 2019

ABOUT THE AUTHOR

Richale R. Reed MA, LCMHCS, LCAS is more than a Licensed Clinical Mental Health Counselor Supervisor, Licensed Clinical Addiction Specialist, Speaker, CEO, Author, Podcast Host, and Coach. She is a Lifework Specialist with more then 30+ years of navigating through her own storms of life. Having undergone a myriad of challenges from childhood trauma, food addiction, and poverty, to the effects of mental illness, academic failures, and rejection; Richale has overcome in a celebratory fashion. In her quest to remain fit and strong to face the realities of life, she has transformed losing and maintaining a weight loss of over 100 pounds. She credits this body transformation to a daily transformation and renewal of the mind. The embodiment of a transformational therapist and life coach Richale has impacted the lives of thousands through her work, bringing a renewed sense of clarity and purpose to their lives.

Richale has a Master's Degree in Professional Christian Counseling from Liberty University. She is the CEO of both CateRRRflies Lifework PLLC, which provides therapeutic services and Empower You Coaching Wealth & Wellness Solutions LLC, offering life and wealth solutions as she is a multi-state independent insurance broker. Richale is a sought-after keynote, conference speaker, and trainer who has also been featured in SheKnows, Comcast, Source Nation, Blog Talk Radio, and more to come.

MORE FROM THE AUTHOR...

2024

Please enjoy my other titles listed below
on Amazon.com

A Black Butterfly's Journey Towards CLAR.R.R.ITY: Rae Rae Versus The Anoroc Virus (2020). This book is the children's version to help your loved ones build resilience and prayer as a coping skill. Includes workbook pages in back.

Silhouette of Her Naked &
Unashamed: A Poetic Journey of
Faith. *(2016) this is a collection*
of poems during some of my most
difficult days where God was still
in the midst of all my troubles
and lessons learned from each
storm.